This book was made especially for...

Sophia

Dear Sophia,

You are *everything* to me! From your smile to your laugh to your giggles and toes, I simply can't imagine life without you. Here's a story to help you understand just how precious you are— and what Everything really means.

Love,

"Sophia,
did you know you're
my Everything?"
said Big Fox one
evening.

"You tell me all the time!" said Sophia.
"But what *is* Everything?"

"Oh, Everything is the best thing you could be. It's every new *flower* that blooms in spring."

"And every drop of *rain* that cools the summer."

"It's what it feels like to ride down the longest *hill* in the world. "

"Or to float up to the highest clouds in the *sky*."

"Everything is *warmer* than the softest penguin in the snow."

"And **stronger** than the tallest llama in the jungle."

"Everything is *big* enough to hold all the new friends your heart could ask for."

"And *small* enough to carry with you everywhere you go."

"Everything means,
'I love you with all
my heart.' On your
happy days . . ."

"... and on your *hard* days."

"And it means I will *always* be there during the long, long nights."

"Best of all,
Everything lasts
forever—longer,
even, than the longest
story that was ever
written."

"Wow," breathed Sophia. There was a comforting silence.

Then Sophia whispered, "If Everything means all that, then *you're my Everything, too.*"

Dearest Sophia, you are my Everything in so many ways! Here are just a few:

_____

_____

_____

_____

_____

_____

_____

_____

_____

_____

Cover and book design by David Miles

Visual credits: animal illustrations (Elena Barenbaum/Shutterstock.com); pink and green flower border (Karma3/Shutterstock.com); green leaves border (mika48/Shutterstock.com); colorful flower border (oksanka007/Shutterstock.com); yellow daisy flower border (TonTonic/Shutterstock.com); blue flower border (elsabenaa/Shutterstock.com); poppy flower border (OlgaVinokurova_art/Shutterstock.com); rose hip and twig flower border (Eisfrei/Shutterstock.com); fall flower border (Gluiki/Shutterstock.com); tropical flower border (Yana Fefelova/Shutterstock.com); snowflake border (Tokarchuk Andrii/Shutterstock.com); balloon border (Anastasia Lembrik/Shutterstock.com); apple flower border (julagaladriel/Shutterstock.com); raindrop border (Xansa/Shutterstock.com); red and blue flower border (Qvasimodo art/Shutterstock.com); clouds (Anna Konchits/Shutterstock.com); water puddle (Cute art/Shutterstock.com); cover stars (Margarita Manish/Shutterstock.com); cover star background (Anna Kutukova/Shutterstock.com); purple, red, and orange watercolor background (Jolliolly/Shutterstock.com); green and blue streaked watercolor background (Jolliolly/Shutterstock.com); green and blue watercolor background (Rennes/Shutterstock.com); cloud watercolor background (Magenta10/Shutterstock.com); blue watercolor background (Alyushin/Shutterstock.com); yellow and orange watercolor background (foxie/Shutterstock.com).

Made in United States
Orlando, FL
02 December 2024

54627395R00020